Oil Spill

TRICIA OKTOBER

Hodder
Children's
Books
Australia

Along the rocky coves and sandy dunes of the southern coast of Australia, live the smallest penguins in the world: the fairy penguins.

Large numbers of fairy penguins live together in colonies, each pair raising one or two chicks a year.

The penguins share their home with many other creatures. Every spring and autumn, flocks of endangered Cape Barren geese fly over the penguins' rookeries, winging their way to and from summer feeding grounds.

On calm afternoons, black-faced cormorants and crested terns fish close inshore, feeding on small fish. The terns dive into the water with a small splash, then, shaking the water from their feathers, fly up and off.

The cormorants stand like scarecrows, holding their wings out to dry in the warm sunshine.

Fur seals gather on the beaches and rocks in summer. They make a deafening noise, with cows bellowing, pups bleating and big bull seals roaring their battle cry of huff, huff, huff.

The huge bull seal claims his piece of territory and stands guard. Mothers and pups recognise each other amongst the crowd by their own particular calls.

Fur seals were once hunted for their skins until they were nearly extinct. They are now a protected species.

Silver gulls and bad-tempered skuas wheel and turn, feeding on anything washed up along the shoreline. The gulls fight with each other for every morsel of food they scavenge. The skuas get most of their food by harrassing the gulls and other sea birds, forcing them to give up their catch.

Gulls and skuas are the penguins' enemies. The large birds attack the tiny penguins and try to steal their eggs and chicks.

For safety against attacks, the little penguins nest underground, digging their burrows beneath clumps of tussock grass or in rocky crevices.

The nesting burrow is lined with dried seaweed or grass, and two small white eggs are hatched. For two months the chicks stay in the warm burrow and are fed by both parents.

The penguins move around the rookery only under cover of darkness.

Fairy penguins are defenceless on land, and only their speed in the water can save them at sea.

They get all their power from their short, strong flippers, with which they "fly" through the water. Their heavy webbed feet act as rudders and their small, plump bodies are streamlined, with stiff, close-packed, waterproof feathers. The little penguins travel underwater, leaping to the surface in graceful arcs to breathe.

Fairy penguins eat pilchards and other small fish, rounding up schools of fish and diving into the middle of them. Snapping their beaks left and right, they swallow their meal underwater.

They go far out to sea for two or three days and return during the night. They gather in the surf, yapping like small puppies, as they prepare to return with a fishy meal for their chicks left sheltering in the burrows.

While chasing fish, the fairy penguins often see huge whales and their calves swimming north to warmer waters, and dolphins chasing cuttlefish.

Despite their vast size, the whales do not hunt fish. Instead, they have a sieve of horny plate in their mouth, which filters the sea water, trapping tiny creatures for them to eat.

Overhead, enormous white-capped albatrosses follow the underwater path of the dolphins. Gliding on wind currents, the birds watch every movement of the fast-moving sea mammals feeding below, waiting until some left-over food appears, then swooping to catch it.

For all the creatures of this rocky coastline, a constant danger is the weather. Violent storms lash land and sea, sometimes driving ships off-course...

As winter sets in, black clouds gather and roll across the sky. In the distance thunder rumbles. Fierce gales whip the high dark sea to a shrieking fury. Heavy waves pound and batter a large ship struggling along the coast. Suddenly, a distress call goes through to the mainland:

OIL SPILL!

Hundreds of tonnes of greasy black fuel oil are pouring from the ship's damaged tanks. It spreads quickly, driven by strong winds and carried by the currents towards the shore. In just a few hours, the tide washes a thick blanket of oil over the beach, leaving it black and ugly. In time, the storm passes, but the oil has been spread far and wide.

Many penguins stay out at sea while the storm rages. It is too dangerous to return and risk being hurled against the shoreline rocks.

As darkness falls, the exhausted little birds begin returning to the rookery. Near shore they surface into pools of floating oil. Their neat navy and white feathers are soaked in the filthy sludge.

Penguins that have stayed in their burrows during the storm are hungry now. They waddle down to the dirty beach and into the pools of floating oil. Soon the beach and rookery are full of cold, shivering, little birds, calling frantically in their distress: yap, yap, yap – yap, yap.

News of the oil spill spreads quickly and by early morning volunteers are being organised to find all the wildlife affected by this disaster. Oil destroys the natural waterproofing of birds and animals, causing them to drown or die of cold, so they must be helped swiftly.

Mopping up the oil begins at once. Clean-up equipment is flown to the area and special chemicals used to disperse the oil. Teams of experts begin skimming oil and placing floating mats on the water to prevent the oil spreading further.

Oil sludge is poisonous to all marine creatures. Some, such as fur seals and dolphins, cannot be helped. Fur seals swim too fast and dive too deep to be rescued. Dolphins are found only when they are beyond help.

Sea birds drenched in oil cannot fly. They are captured and cared for.

Cormorants and fairy penguins are most at risk; whole colonies can be wiped out. But there is hope: volunteers take turns to search, day and night, in the icy winds. With rubber-gloved hands, they scoop up the squawking, nipping little birds, to place them in cardboard carry boxes.

At the rescue centre, vets treat the frightened birds, wiping ointment around their sore eyes.

Waterlogged and chilled, the little birds waiting to be washed are wrapped in small warm jackets hurriedly made from scraps of cloth and sticky tape. The jackets stop the birds cleaning their feathers and swallowing the poisonous oil.

In a dish of warm water and detergent, every little penguin in turn is slowly and carefully cleaned, until all the deadly oil has been removed. Their dark blue and white plumage is once again revealed as the oil is slowly washed away.

Then they are wiped, and thoroughly dried with warm air from a hairdrier. Again the little penguins are closely inspected by vets and are treated for any oil they may have swallowed.

The birds are tube-fed with a glucose mixture. A few hours later, they can eat by themselves, but will have to stay in captivity until their feathers are again waterproof and seaworthy.

Many months will pass before all traces of oil have disappeared from the disaster area. But the immediate danger to wildlife has been swiftly dealt with, and at last the day arrives when the rescued penguins can be tested for seaworthiness.

One evening the first birds are released at sea. As darkness falls over the rookery and the moon rises high, the first puppy-like yaps are heard. It is the gathering call of fairy penguins travelling home from the sea.

A group of little birds, their white breasts gleaming in the moonlight, come wading through the lace of sea-foam and up the beach. Small and plump, with flippers held out for balance, they make their way over the sand and up into the safety of the grass and scrub of the rookery. They are the little web-footed fairies that have survived.

NOTES FOR PARENTS AND TEACHERS

For the last thirty years, naturalists and conservationists have warned of ships discharging oil illegally along the coasts. This practice is now carefully monitored and heavy penalties imposed on offenders.

However, accidents do occur, and ships grounding on rocky coastlines have resulted in major oil spills in other parts of the world. Of necessity, environmentalists have had to learn swiftly how to deal with the effects such disasters have on the eco-system.

The effects of an oil spill are felt worldwide. For example, many sea birds from the northern hemisphere are migratory and spend the winter months along Australia's coast. When such birds are killed as a result of an oil spill, the numbers of birds migrating to Australia are reduced.

Other sea creatures are restricted to small areas of coast and an oil spill can lead to some species becoming extinct. Fairy penguins are particularly vulnerable as they inhabit only the southern coast of Australia and the west coast of New Zealand.

With Australia's vast coastline it is only a matter of time before a disaster of massive destruction happens. It would be comforting to know that we have the organisation and technology in place to deal swiftly with such an accident.

For Graham Pizzey
Australian naturalist, wildlife
photographer and writer

A Hodder Children's Book

Published in Australia and New Zealand in 1996
by Hodder Headline Australia Pty Limited,
(A member of the Hodder Headline Group)
10-16 South Street, Rydalmere NSW 2116

First published in paperback 1999
Reprinted 1999 (twice)

National Library of Australia Cataloguing-in-Publication data

Oktober, Tricia.
Oil Spill.

ISBN 0 7336 0936 8
I. Title.
A823.3

Printed in Hong Kong